Maryam's Maze

Maryam's Maze

Mansoura Ez Eldin

Translated by Paul Starkey

The American University in Cairo Press
Cairo   New York

First published in 2007 by
The American University in Cairo Press
113 Sharia Kasr el Aini, Cairo, Egypt
420 Fifth Avenue, New York, NY 10018
www.aucpress.com

First paperback edition 2009

An extract from this novel appeared in *Banipal: Magazine of Modern Arabic Literature*
No. 25, Spring 2006.

Dar el Kutub No. 4202/09
ISBN 978 977 416 308 1

Dar el Kutub Cataloging-in-Publication Data

Ez Eldin, Mansoura
        Maryam's Maze / Mansoura Ez Eldin; translated by Paul Starkey.—Cairo:
    The American University in Cairo Press, 2009
            p.   cm.
            ISBN 977 416 308 7
            1. Arabic fiction   I. Starkey, Paul (Trans.) II. Title
            892.73

1 2 3 4 5 6 7 8   14 13 12 11 10 09

Designed by Fatiha Bouzidi/AUC Press Design Center
Printed in Egypt

The story goes that when El Tagi decided to build his palace, he brought several pieces of flesh, scattered them over various pieces of ground, and then chose the spot that had kept the flesh from rotting for the longest time. There he built his magnificent palace with its domes and marble façades. He wanted it to be unlike any other building, so he filled it with as many cellars and corridors as he could, as well as spacious halls and windows with colored glass, and wide balconies edged with low walls topped with black balustrades shaped like tree branches ending in silver flowers. These balustrades also supported the jasmine shrubs whose fragrance rocked the place, enveloping it in a disturbing smell that on hot summer afternoons turned into a curse for those with sensitive chests, making them gasp for breath.

They say that if someone dies in a dream after a fatal blow, he will be killed at the same moment in the real world. In the same way, if someone falls from a great height and hits the ground in a dream, his heart will stop immediately. How is it that Maryam was still living, then? There was another woman of roughly her age, with her face and her body, walking beside her. They went into a big house together . . . in fact, it wasn't just a house—it was a palace. Maryam remembers now that she could hear her companion's heartbeats. Something was making them feel afraid. The place was like an endless maze, full of closed rooms and halls that led into each other in a way that reminded her of El Tagi's palace, and all the disturbing memories that it represented. They went up or down three flights of stairs, moving from one large room to another until they reached their destination, where they found themselves standing on a high balcony. A hundred yards below, there was a hall that seemed to be made of red brass, with a table in it surrounded by several gold-colored chairs.

Maryam could not look down. She felt that she was standing on a fine wire separating two lofty mountains. Suddenly they started to appear, like ghosts.

Strange phantoms, ghosts of everyone she had met in her life, were walking slowly along, their faces wearing dumb expressions. The sudden appearance of these phantoms terrified her unexpectedly. Something about them was different from the real people they represented, making them seem more like evil spirits conspiring against her. The balcony shook and she found herself alone among the phantoms, which quickly started to evaporate, disappearing as if they had never existed, leaving behind them nothing but spots of coagulated blood.

The other girl came back again. She looked forcefully into Maryam's eyes before the word 'murder' floated into their minds. It began as if Maryam was witnessing a crime; as if someone she knew well had killed someone dear to her. The sensation hurt her a lot, but the pain did not last long, as, together with her companion, she busied herself with washing away the blood that was sticking to the floor. For some reason, the girl then stabbed her several times, making Maryam's blood pour out. Then the girl began to writhe about just like Maryam until she too fell down dead beside her.

When Maryam woke up, she was astonished to find herself among the living. She thought that she must have been given another life. She was suffering from a terrible headache, and the visitors of her dream weighed heavily on her mind. She tried to ignore them. She was conscious, perhaps for the first time, of being in the wrong place. She was supposed to be waking up in her bed in the narrow room at the girls' hostel with the gray paint flaking in several places and pictures torn out of magazines stuck carelessly on the walls with little pieces of sticky tape. Instead, she was now lying on an enormous bed that gripped her body like a pair of handcuffs. Everything around her suggested age: the bed with its raised decorations, the wardrobe with the broken door leaf, and the dressing table with the murky mirror, not to mention the trunk made of sandalwood and decorated with shells, most of them broken.

She didn't bother to examine the place closely. What baffled her was that she couldn't remember how she had come to be here—the Abdin flat, as they called it—which no one had set foot in since Yusif had graduated from the College of Pharmacy and returned to El Tagi's palace.

She shook off her feeling of laziness and stood up to explore her new surroundings. To her great surprise, she found her clothes hanging undisturbed in the wardrobe, as if they had never been anywhere else. Her cosmetics were carefully arranged in rows in the dressing table drawers, and some of her hair was still stuck between the teeth of a brown comb, while her papers were scattered around on the dining room table and the chairs in the dilapidated entrance hall. In the bathroom, a piece of soap was nestled in the soap holder.

She went into the kitchen, where she was surprised to see some leftovers in dishes. In the fridge she found a container of cheese and some slices of luncheon meat, with nine eggs, a bottle of mineral water, and some tomatoes and sweet peppers. The sink was filled to the brim with dirty dishes.

Everything about the place suggested that she had been living there for a while, though her fragile memory kept telling her that she had gone to bed the previous day in the room with the foul smell that she lived in at the girls' hostel. She had read a letter that Radwa had left for her in the room, informing her that she had left the place and would not be coming back. She held her head in her right hand and went back to the bedroom. She opened the window and as she was turning around to move away from it, she came face to face with herself in the murky dressing table mirror. Her heart almost stopped beating. It wasn't her face as she knew it. Something about it had changed—there was either something new there, or else something had gone. It didn't matter; it no longer concerned her.

She lay down on the bed for she didn't know how long. She was incapable of thinking about anything. Snapshots of her life passed in front of her in a random, disjointed way, without adding up to a complete or coherent picture. There were lots of gaps that she just couldn't fill.

"I'm nobody," said Maryam, but it wasn't like the usual scene in a bad detective story, when the wicked villain shouts: "Nobody will defeat me," and the hero replies with confident scorn: "I am nobody."

Unlike those people, who propped themselves up with a quite outrageous conviction, Maryam felt that she had been reduced to nothingness. She no longer had any physical existence to fill a space in the void. From this moment on, she had to face the world like someone experiencing life for the first time. She grabbed her handbag from the bedside table and tipped out its contents onto the bed. Her hand trembled as she went through what was in it: some small pieces of paper folded up carelessly, an identity card with a picture of herself on it, smiling doltishly with her new features, Radwa's letter, and some photographs with yellowing edges. She got dressed and went out quickly. In the street, the wind was so strong that she felt it penetrating her pores, forcing her backward against her will. She walked with difficulty along the streets in the city center, defying the particles in the heavy air, trying to ignore the sights and faces that came into her mind like ghosts only to immediately disappear. Eventually, she found herself walking slowly along Suq el Tawfiqiya Street. She ignored the harsh, clashing voices as she stared at a point in space in front of her eyes. There was a man splashing water in front of his shop. A fruit seller was busy beating the flies off his fruit, and the sound of a radio could be clearly heard from a neighboring café. As she pushed her way with difficulty through the crowd, she imagined that she was walking in a movie, or in some other existence. She wanted to touch the fruit seller's peaches and mangoes to convince herself that things were real. Why was she being pursued by this deadly sensation that she was floating on top of the world without living in it, and that the world itself only existed in her imagination?

The weather was extremely hot. She lifted her hair clear off her neck, which was damp with warm sweat. As she sat in an out-of-the-way corner of the café on Alfy Street, she hoped that she wouldn't have to wait for Yahya for long. She was wakened from her musings by the sound of an offensive word from the mouth of one of a group of youths sitting around a neighboring table. She fiddled with the silver ring on her finger, obviously nervous. The youths winked at each other and started to compete to see who could make the rudest comments. Maryam looked at her watch and found that it was five in the afternoon. Her appointment with Yahya had been at four. She left quietly. When she tried to ring him later, she was answered by the metallic voice of the telephone operator: "This number is not in service. Please check the correct number and try again." She tried to phone more than once, but she always got the same reply. She decided to visit him at his workplace.

The office was almost empty. There were only two people in it, bent over their work. They were people that Maryam had never seen before, even though she had been coming to the place for a very long time. She cleared her throat audibly, and one of them looked up at her.

"Excuse me, is Mister Yahya here?"

"Yahya who?"

"Yahya el Gindi."

"You mean Hazim el Gindi?"

"No . . . Yahya. I know him well. He works here."

"There's no one here with that name."

He said it sharply, even a little angrily, and bent over his papers again. She was forced to leave without understanding what lay behind the aggressiveness of the man's reply. When she got back to the apartment, she turned everything in it upside down until she found the copies she was keeping of the newspaper that Yahya worked on. She leafed through them like a maniac, looking for his name or some articles by him. Some issues went back three years. She went through every word in them without success. She strewed the copies around her and left them lying on the floor. She burst into a stream of bitter tears punctuated by stifled screams until she fell into a deep sleep.

She woke up in the afternoon of the following day, determined to reach Radwa. She picked up her jeans and put them on quickly, with a white T-shirt with a picture of Che Guevara in his military uniform. Her hair was disheveled, and her face looked ugly and pale without any makeup. She slung her canvas bag over her shoulder and went out running.

When she left the taxi that had brought her to the hostel, her heart was leaping in her chest with anxiety. She opened the metal door to the building, and bounded up the staircase, which was almost dark. She couldn't find the switch for the staircase light until she reached the second floor. She stood in front of the warden's door and pressed the bell. She expected to be confronted by the old woman's childlike face, but no one opened the door. She pressed the bell several times, then continued climbing up. She took out her keys and unlocked the door, which opened in front of her. She found herself facing the hallway exactly as she had imagined it. There was nothing in it except for a worn-out refrigerator, probably dating back to the sixties, the noise of whose motor drowned out everything else. The walls had probably started out blue, but they had turned dark gray with the passage of time. Pretending to be calm, Maryam undid the lock to her room. She had often looked at the lock as a mere message from Radwa—if the lock was there, it meant that Radwa was not there, and if the lock was gone, then Radwa would be inside. Now, Radwa had evaporated from the space within the room and there was no longer any evidence of her. Maryam examined the place carefully, but couldn't see any of either her or Radwa's things. There were some strange pictures stuck to the walls, and everything was in total chaos, with the remains of some milky tea in two glasses on the floor of the room. Before Maryam went out, abandoning herself to the state of total paralysis that had taken hold of her mind, she noticed a sentence written in colored chalk and shaky English letters at the top of the wall opposite—"Dead man walking, dead man talking." It was Radwa's favorite song, and it was written in her own handwriting, with the chalk that she always used to write graffiti on the walls. Maryam recalled that only two days previously, she had waked at five in the morning to the sound of shrill shouts, in which she could make out Radwa's voice arguing with the warden. She hadn't come back by the time Maryam went to bed, so Maryam had thought that she would be away for several days as she usually was. The shouting gradually started to turn into definite words, with insults and curses jumping from one topic to another. The words became even clearer when they left the landing and went into the empty hallway. Maryam pretended to be asleep. She was shocked by the vulgar expressions flying like bullets from Radwa's mouth.

"Stop it. I can't take it any more! You've driven me crazy with this grubby flat of yours. I'm not staying here any more!" Radwa shouted.

"You should thank God that I've kept quiet about you," replied the woman. "Is this my reward for not exposing you?"

This last sentence struck Maryam like a thunderbolt, especially when the woman's voice got even louder and she started reeling off the details of Radwa's relationships with other people . . . precise details that Maryam had known nothing about and hadn't even imagined, despite her own supposedly deep relationship with Radwa.

This was the same Radwa who as a young girl used to set the dial on the radio to Voice of America, listening to a lot of chatter that gave Maryam a headache, and dancing noisily to the rhythms of hard rock tunes. Suddenly she would listen intently, and almost stop breathing when his voice flowed over the ether waves. She would prick up her ears to catch each fluctuation of sound, searching for the words that concerned her. But she never reached them. The voice would change into a public voice aimed at thousands of listeners who followed it over the shortwaves as the man read out the names of friends of the program, dedicated songs to people who the radio abbreviated to mere letters uttered into the void, and cracked jokes he thought amusing. Radwa would switch off the radio angrily, walk back and forth between the two beds, then switch it on again, just to listen to the voice of her father who worked for the Voice of America and sent her money at the start of each month, and a postcard with "Kisses to my little Radwa" and nothing else written on it.

Now Maryam started to imitate Radwa. She would not turn the dial on the radio away from Voice of America as she waited for the man's voice. She was desperate for him to supply her with any news about his daughter. As usual, though, it was just a general voice with no depth to speak of, ramming home his boorish commentary and leaving Maryam on the verge of madness.

A short while after he had built the palace, the wheels of El Tagi's carriage crushed the body of one of his servants. The congealed blood formed a pool like a small lake before it eventually dried, sticking to the ground. For many years nothing succeeded in removing the traces of that blood.

T he bougainvillea tree with its thick shadows could not disguise the heavy stench of death that was making its way relentlessly into the place. The Peugeot stopped in the pathway in front of the outer stairs leading up to the palace. Barriers of silence enveloped the place, as Narges, with Maryam beside her, stared at the strange car through the window overlooking the veranda. Four men wearing black cloaks over their cashmere gallabiyas stepped from the hearse and opened the door at the rear. They took out a body wrapped in a white sheet and carried it up the steps. Narges's heart was racing as she caught a glimpse of Yusif's shoes visible beneath the white cloth. She screamed with all the fear that she harbored deep inside her, as the four men went in, fortified by the confidence lent them by death. Their feet plied the ground of the palace that they had often been afraid even to approach. Narges's screams brought together the servants around her, although as usual Zaynab didn't leave her place, where years ago she had become almost desiccated.

Narges insisted that Yusif's body should lie on her bed. She turned everyone out and shut the door on the two of them.

While the people outside busied themselves with preparations for the forthcoming funeral procession, she bent over his face that had turned blue. She pulled off his damp clothes, careful to avoid looking at the multiple bruises spread over a body that had throbbed with life only a short time before. A pool of congealed blood had collected in his left ear. His silver ring, decorated with a turquoise stone from Sinai, looked like an amulet to attract death. She did not give in to the increasing number of knocks on the door. She burst into tears as she embraced his naked body, from which life had now passed forever. For the first time she felt that she possessed him completely and that he had become completely hers, out of reach of Kawthar's love. But what could she take from him now? She couldn't hold on to him forever. She screamed when she realized that the person she held between her hands was no longer Yusif el Tagi. He had stopped being the person she had married the moment his soul left the lifeless body with no left arm that lay before her. She knew that the car had overturned on its way to Kawthar's, but that did not bother her now. For the first time, she was acknowledging the existence of that woman, even conceding to the fact that Yusif belonged to her. The thoughts piled up inside her head. She felt her head burning and collapsed in a faint beside him. She was completely unaware of the door being forced open under the weight of the bodies pushing it.

An enormous tent had been set up on the open ground and was completely full of mourners. Saleh, Narges's father, who loved funerals, stood in the middle of it. It made Zaynab weep and wail, although she had not left the house since morning.

She was weeping for El Tagi's lost glory, and for his other son who had been killed. If either had been alive, he would have been sitting instead of strangers to accept the condolences for Yusif. Zaynab's shrieking continued like the hooting of an owl, stirring terror in people's hearts. People heard her and thought that she was mourning her husband's son, who had died when his car overturned in the water. No one realized that she was weeping in the first place for herself.

When Zaynab had gone into El Tagi's palace for the first time, she thought that she had taken possession of the whole universe. She brought with her the resounding reputation of an influential family, but she was dazzled by El Tagi's intimidating personality, by his magnificent palace, and by the extensive fruit orchards that he owned. Something in his lifestyle told her that he was far superior to her family's wealth. She took no notice of the fact that he was married to the woman called Sofia. When she saw her, she realized that she didn't represent any danger worth speaking of, and that the man would be hers, with no competition from that woman, whom everyone thought aloof and remote, living in a different world from the one they were familiar with.

Immediately after the afternoon prayer, just as Yusif's funeral procession was about to set off, everyone was startled by the heavy steps of Sofia's ghost resounding from the area to the rear of the palace. As usual, it walked extremely noisily. It began to wander through the palace trying to open the doors. They reckoned it was looking for Yusif. Although Sofia had been mad, her ghost seemed extremely intelligent. The ponderous footsteps went out into the garden, following the noise of the shrieking, and finally reached the tent outside. When the procession moved off, the mourners were conscious of the footsteps following them. Sofia's ghost walked behind them, pounding the earth with its feet. When they laid Yusif's body in the ground, finished the Quran recitation, and set off back, the ghost remained in front of the entrance to the tomb, and passersby heard the sound of two hands beating on the door that was not yet dry, and the noise of weeping rising from the spot.

At the start of Sofia's marriage to El Tagi, he had hit her hard on her face. She had tried to avoid him and the blows struck her right ear. From that moment, Sofia had lost her hearing in that ear and had taken to walking with heavy steps that left a great clatter behind her. Later, her ghost had started to walk leaving the same noise behind it, as if it too was suffering from deafness.

It was quite understandable that the ghost should be walking about in the palace, but it was illogical for Maryam to feel the ghost pursuing her wherever she went.

In the hours at the end of the night, when the girls' hostel was empty except for herself, Maryam would hear heavy footsteps and feet moving with a great ruckus. Almost dying of fright, she would hide herself under the covers with the light on. At once, her old image of Sofia would disappear from her mind, turning into nothing but some enormous feet that made a continuous clatter, before suddenly retreating, leaving Maryam terrified, constantly shaking and weeping.

She was alone chasing a wisdom that she both sought and knew she would reach. Maryam would recall it later as something fevered and painful, perhaps as a future that awaited her eagerly. No sooner would the door open than she would hurl herself through it to try to catch the papers strewn in the streets and to search in the piles of rubbish for things that no one but she knew. She would disappear for the entire late morning and end up wandering along one of the paths between the tombs, then fall asleep exhausted. She would come back with bunches of mint and sweet basil, and broad succulent leaves oozing with a bitter, sticky liquid. Her palm would be saturated with the juice, so that when she later brought it up to her eyes, she would sit crying like a child, rubbing her eyes hard, until Narges dragged her to her room and gave her a sleeping pill. "Your mother will embarrass us," she would whisper to Yusif, and he would look at the ceiling without replying.

A few hours after Yusif's burial, Narges suffered a violent nervous collapse. She succumbed to the injection of tranquilizers that the doctor gave her and sank into a deep sleep. The palace turned into a busy beehive. Every lamp was lit and the servants crowded into the kitchen to prepare the food. Zaynab stood there, once again the young woman, supervising and shouting at them. She sent back all the trays that had arrived loaded with delicacies from important local families, and ordered beasts to be slaughtered at her own expense and enough food to be prepared for everyone in the village.

Despite Yusif el Tagi's tragic end, there was a sort of pleasure mingled with the sorrow in the hearts of the servants and others working in the palace. For several years, it had been a sort of wasteland, but with the death of its owner it was now buzzing with life. The lighted lamps and the state of delightful chaos took them back to the days of the great El Tagi, to the days when the rich and noble used to gather in one of the great halls under the friendly protection first of the light of the mantle lamps, then the more artificial one of the electricity generators.

On the morning of the day Yusif died, Kawthar woke early. She tidied her house and prepared for Yusif the food that he liked, with two packets of Marlboro Red cigarettes. Then she put some bottles of beer in the fridge.

A slight tremor in her heart told her that he would not be coming to her again. She moved slowly, letting her eyes wander around the titles in her small library, before taking down the first volume of *The Thousand and One Nights*. By reading it, she would try to outwit time, until her ears picked up the sound of the screech of his blue car's wheels.

In a house surrounded by a hedge of lemon trees overgrown with ivy branches that almost strangled them, sat a woman called Kawthar. She was struggling against the smell of death that she felt close to her. She was totally absorbed in the story of a mythical king and his wife who fended off death with endless tales of enchanted kings and youths, and of sprites who floated in the skies above the cities.

For some moments she forgot everything that concerned her. Eventually, though, she was forced to push the book to one side and begin wandering around her house. Her feeling of restlessness had no excuse, for it was unlikely that Yusif would visit her so early—though, as he had assured her that he would, she had waked early to receive him.

She took a bottle of beer out of the refrigerator and gulped down the contents without bothering to get a glass. When the bottle fell, smashing into hundreds of tiny pieces, Kawthar flung herself onto a nearby armchair and burst into tears.

She had persuaded herself that Yusif was her destiny, from which there was no escape. She did not ask him for anything. To him, she seemed quite the opposite of Narges, with her never-ending complaints and demands. She wasn't any prettier than her and there was nothing to distinguish her from Narges except for her inscrutability, on which she was heavily dependent, as if she knew that it was her private myth. She was simultaneously the complement and the double of Yusif. He always compared her to a dangerous gambler who might gamble on his own life.

What is it that ties me to him? thought Kawthar. For the first time in their relationship she was troubled by the thought that here was a new person whom she would not be able to do without, and that she would be badly hurt if he left her or went away leaving her alone. It was the same feeling she had had about her brother after their father's death, a feeling that had led her to destroy his image inside her for fear of the pain that his loss would cause; the same feeling that she had had about her ex-husband at the start of their marriage, before their life together cooled. She had lived her whole life constantly seeking to avoid involvement, even though she had been unaware of it. And now here was Yusif's late arrival throwing her at the mercy of her old anxieties.

Afterward, when she learned the news of his death, she shut the door of her house on herself, and for a long time no one saw her outside it. There was no one who could console her. Even though everyone knew of her relationship with him, no one would dare to expose it, or shift the relationship from the realm of secrecy to public view, even through a sympathetic glance. Even death could not break this barrier of conspiracy.

The first thing that Kawthar wanted to do when she emerged from her several months of seclusion was to meet Narges. She sent several letters to her via her maid Nur, but Narges persisted in refusing her rival's invitation.

When she finally gave in, in the face of Kawthar's stubborn insistence, almost a year had gone by since Yusif's death.

Curiosity was a basic motive. As the days went by, and her rival continued to be just as insistent, Narges's curiosity was gradually aroused. She wanted to learn the secret of that powerful, even overpowering, desire to meet her. What was it that the other woman wanted from her?

She received her on the terrace, as though unwilling to allow her to penetrate any further into her private world. She was expecting that Kawthar would show her an official marriage certificate or something like that, but she did not do anything of the sort. She gave the impression that these things did not concern her at all. She just stared at Narges from head to toe, with a curiosity mingled with caution. Her eyes took in everything about Narges: a few small white hairs where her hair was parted; the silver varnish on her nails; the black bra that was visible through her thin white dress; the look of defeat that from time to time floated lightly across the surface of her eyes; and the way she picked at her nose with her thumb and forefinger when she was tense.

Kawthar talked about wanting to leave the village, about her son and her short, miserable marriage, but she avoided mentioning anything about Yusif apart from telling Narges as she was leaving that Yusif loved his family a lot.

It was with some difficulty that Narges restrained herself from asking her rival the question that had often kept her awake: "Does Yusif say anything when he is making love to you, or does he keep silent?"

El Tagi was a keen ear picking up even the smallest sounds from the various parts of the palace, and a penetrating eye that took in the smallest details of the scenes that he saw. In short, he was a curse on two legs.

Yusif watches the world from behind the glass of his spectacles, his wide eyes moving slowly. They seem even wider when he raises his eyebrows, as if wanting to take in the whole scene—though at other times, he seems like someone who does not see what he is looking at, but who is simply hiding behind his glasses.

He arranges the medicines in his little chemist's shop, muttering a few unintelligible words. From time to time he listens to the stream of sounds emerging brightly from the radio, while Maryam sits absentmindedly on a chair next to his desk, counting her fingers and trying to repeat the songs she has learned in school. She stops abruptly as Yusif looks at her sharply, whenever her voice rises above the permitted level, then immerses herself in her private silence. To the customers, they seem like two people competing for silence.

Maryam's wide eyes follow the passersby in the street through the door that is always open. The boys and girls who play with her pass and wave to her, but she behaves as if she does not know them, looking away toward Yusif who is intent on reading the newspapers. She doesn't know what to do with her hands. Should she put them down beside her without moving them, or should she move them very slowly, as if getting used to their being there? She only feels they are of any use when Yusif drags her by the hand on the way back home, when he has left without the car. Then she walks beside him, looking at the ground, feeling strangely embarrassed, and hoping that her friends will not see her with him. She doesn't want to give them tangible proof that she is a daughter of that family. She has never admitted that Yusif's missing arm has anything to do with it.

Right from the beginning, she had noticed that he insisted on doing everything by himself. He ate, combed his hair, lit his cigarette, and even drove his car with his one hand. Narges didn't often press him, but left him as he liked to be, having already wasted a considerable amount of her life trying to help him. When she gave up in despair, she turned her concern to Maryam instead, and devoted herself to her completely.

Yusif el Tagi was a made up name, invented to make him sound like an aristocrat or a hero. But what does heroism mean? Is it like the scenarios that Maryam made up to excuse the absence of Yusif's other arm? "He lost it on the front line," she would repeat in a voice of exaggerated seriousness and gloom when she noticed a questioning look in the eyes of her friends. They would fall completely silent under the weight of the words that Maryam used to lash them with, and seek no further explanation. She gradually became used to seeing his empty left sleeve, but she never dared to look at the stump of his missing arm. She would watch him cleaning his ancient rifle without saying a word, and he would rock it and fondle it like a young child. He would spend many hours with it while Maryam hovered around him, without paying her any attention. She never argued. She never asked which front it was that had done that to him. The threads gradually came together in her mind without her trying to pull them together, and she left them in a sort of knotted but unconnected bunch. She would see the small brown lumps that Narges found in his pockets and which made her start to wail. She would go with him to shabby drug dens, understanding nothing of what went on in them; she saw huge bottles with foreign words and obscure pictures in a small cupboard in his office room without knowing what connection they might have with anything. Maryam does not remember the first time she suddenly fathomed what those things meant: perhaps it was the morning when she heard Narges arguing with him. She was saying something about her, about how dangerous it was for him to take her to those places. She didn't know that they were the only places where Yusif could meet the self that he had one day lost, but lived in hope of meeting again.

If Maryam had wanted to give Yusif a nickname that suited him, she would have chosen 'mystery man.' He loved to camouflage himself, he loved to change color, just so that no one would know what he was thinking about. Was he good or bad? Was he reckless, like a gambler with no heart, or cautious, like a cat? These were all things that were difficult to comprehend. Most likely, his addiction to hashish basically went back to his desire to disappear behind clouds of thick dark smoke. The cramped dens reeking of blue smoke gave him an overwhelming sense of mystery. He would leave them happy and light-headed, surrounded by a halo of mystery which came closer and closer to him until it almost destroyed him.

Like all children, Maryam loved clarity. She never acknowledged gray areas, so she never had the time to understand Yusif or get close to him. He would drag her home behind him from the chemist's shop, to the cafés where he smoked and sometimes to Kawthar's house itself. She would stay with him the whole time, but they were like two trains traveling on parallel tracks in opposite directions to one another.

Kawthar's house was the only thing that was strange to her. Yusif would take her there from time to time. His visits were short and quickly finished, but he would leave Kawthar with a promise to return. Maryam would be overcome with a deep feeling of guilt when Narges asked her "Where did you go with Yusif?" and she would be forced to lie.

She would watch the pale, sturdy Kawthar as she laughed, as she spoke in her hoarse, seductive voice, without understanding the secret of her relationship with Yusif. She just sensed, with her childhood intuition, that there was something not right about it. Otherwise, why would Narges hate the woman? Or why would she go berserk when her name was mentioned?

Contrary to Narges's belief, Kawthar seemed to Maryam a pleasant woman, very kind and gentle. She would give her sweets whenever she went to her house and embrace her hard, laughing as she spoke to Yusif.

Another woman that Narges hated but Maryam was attached to was Nur, Sofia's old servant and Yusif's confidante.

The woman Yusif called Narges never allowed Maryam to utter Nur's name in front of her, and never allowed anyone in the palace even to hint at the existence of Kawthar. For a long time, she had believed that ignoring a thing or a person meant quite simply that it did not exist, and she had therefore gone to great lengths to wipe out any trace of Kawthar. Indeed, since Yusif had left her for the other woman, she had become a different person. She was no longer the radiant young girl who had entered El Tagi's palace for the first time. With the passing of the years, she was starting to resemble the palace itself, full of cellars and snares. Now that Yusif had surrendered completely to the embrace of another woman, she had changed completely from how she had originally been. She paid more attention to detail. She would stand in the kitchen to watch the maid as she prepared the food and ask her about the price of fruit and vegetables with a strange hostility. She would wash the plastic flowers herself and feel the paint on the walls to check that it was sound. Above all, she began to take after Sofia in her attention to the garden, although she did it in a different way. She would water the rose bushes, and the peach, mango, and almond trees forever. She would touch the leaves lovingly, refusing to let the gardener's shears near them for pruning. She left the trees and grass to grow wild and completely out of hand, turning the garden into a miniature jungle. She seemed like someone who wanted to disappear as everything around her grew bigger. As a demonstration of that, she took to sitting in the middle of a small forest of intertwined lemon trees, withdrawn into herself, looking at the horizon before her without a single word. Then she would quickly gather the lemons from the trees in a small basket and put them on the kitchen marble beside the maid, who would ignore the basket and leave it until the fruit dried, while Narges looked on without comment.

She began to count her losses, which had piled up during the years of her marriage. She had known that marriage would make her lose herself, but had nonetheless immersed herself in it totally. She had abandoned her dreams of completing a master's thesis in English literature on William Blake, and occupied herself with the intricacies of El Tagi's family. Only now did she return, like a soldier who had rushed into horrendous battles, only to suddenly discover that the victories had not been credited to him, but rather to his commander.

Yusif knew better than anyone that Narges was in love with herself . . . in love with the young girl of eighteen she had been. She would have liked herself and her experience to have stood still at that age, with her personality at the time. For this reason, despite her love for Yusif, she had never wanted to be totally in love with him, or to immerse herself in him totally. She always looked at him as a person trying to steal from her the girl she had been and whom she still loved.

While she was pregnant with Maryam, Narges realized that she was on the threshold of a frightening experience. She would wake up every morning to stand naked in front of the mirror, watching the developments that were overtaking her body. She would press her belly as if she wanted the intrusive swelling to disappear. She was disturbed by her bosom when it began to grow larger, but she only began really to hate her pregnancy when the pink circles around her nipples began to change to a dark brown color. She realized that she had lost a part of herself that she would never recover. When her belly began to swell further, she started to watch her navel with alarm. It was no longer just a small sunken area in the center of her belly, but began to protrude outward, changing in turn into another smaller swelling in the middle of the bigger swelling.

Narges was scared of the idea that her body might never return to its original way of working. She didn't understand what was happening to it. She hadn't grasped the idea that it was an unstable and fickle thing, beginning with menstruation, pregnancy, childbirth, and then whatever might follow. The transformation had made her lose the pleasure of possessing a solid body unaffected by any fundamental changes; a body that would not betray her, or conspire with Yusif against her to set her in front of another woman with a swollen belly whom she continued to observe in the mirror for seven months.

A month after giving birth to Maryam, Narges woke up to find a column of small black ants crawling up her left arm toward her shoulder. She cried out in horror as she looked at the black thread, massed together and advancing in formation, then ran to the bathroom, abandoning her body to the water despite the freezing winter morning. She searched every inch of her room but found no trace of the ants. She therefore decided to put this sudden incident behind her and surrendered herself to the peaceful rhythm of her life. The following day, however, she was surprised at dawn by an attack even more voracious than the previous one. She felt vicious bites all over her body, and saw vast armies of ants covering her completely. The ants were moving in a series of columns, all heading toward her heart, as if they wanted to devour her. Vicious, devious ants that left no trace outside the boundaries of the space she herself occupied, as if they had sprung from a void with a single purpose that she did not completely understand, but was afraid of even imagining.

Fear drove her to immerse herself completely in the game. She waited for the swarms of ants on the nights that followed, but they didn't come. When she had stopped expecting them, she woke to the sound of a muffled scream in her darkened room to find a small group of ants feeding from her left breast and another covering her mouth. She sat there shuddering with an intense fear.

She believed that the smell of milk in her breasts was attracting the ants, which were waiting for a suitable opportunity to consume her. But she never understood how those persistent creatures emerged to violate her in winter at night. Her body's surrender to the ants' attacks was worse than all its earlier betrayals of her, though at least part of it seemed anxious to understand what was happening and was eager to complete the course to the end. This was despite her intense pain from the continuous bites, and her terror at the muffled shouts she could hear in the pitch dark of her room.

She dreamed that she was walking naked along a dark road. She was hardly aware of her own movement, when suddenly she found herself moving in a pool of light whose borders were formed by giant ants preparing to consume her. Then her body, which had again become beautiful, began to change, each time assuming a form that was completely foreign to her. She raised her left arm to her mouth and began to consume it, oblivious to the blood that was flowing from it. Then she moved to the other arm, to her legs and torso. She slowed as she consumed her trembling heart until she disappeared, leaving behind her a pool of crimson blood that the giant ants licked up until it was all gone.

Narges began to hate her body more than at any time in the past. She looked at the little girl sleeping beside her, trying to convince herself that only one month ago she had been inside her. She felt that her breasts were extremely heavy and that she was unable to do anything about it.

The niggling ache that pricked her, and the little creatures trying to eat her during the night, were of course connected with the milk stored in her breasts. This all increased the alienation she felt from her body. Her problems were further multiplied by the nightmares that assailed her at night, and which all revolved around her losing her child through her gross neglect. Rather than nightmares, it was actually a single nightmare, repeated dozens of times each night. She would see Maryam desperately seeking refuge from the excessive pain. From time to time, loud shrieks would escape from her mouth, shrieks that her tiny heart could hardly bear. Narges would run toward her, wanting to cuddle her, but despite herself she would hold her to her mouth and swallow her at a single gulp, turning herself into her graveyard. She was frightened by the idea of swallowing her baby, but she was at the same time almost as frightened by the idea that her belly would fill with her again. Did this mean that she would be exposed again to the painful experience of childbirth? Did it mean that her daughter would die by her hands? Narges would wake screaming and calm down only when she heard Maryam, who was sleeping beside her, cry out, disturbed by her mother's sudden shouts. She never told anyone about this dream, for fear that it might turn into reality, but she never forgot it for a single moment. Whenever she looked at Maryam, she asked herself what terrible thing she might do to her. This was the only thing that released her from the prison of her self-obsession.

When Sofia died, Narges was at her side, along with Yusif, Nur the maid, and little Maryam. Sofia had turned into a skeleton, giving out foul smells as she waited for her soul to leave her. She began to look around at them in turns, incomprehensible tears suspended in her eyes. From the little group, she chose to fix her gaze on Narges, as if she wanted to tell her something in particular, but she couldn't speak. Death seemed to Narges terrifying and inhuman, but despite that, she wanted to die young and without getting ill. She didn't want to see any more evidence of her body's betrayal. She never wanted to witness it collapse, waste away, or turn into something resembling a corpse, quite remote from the beloved if frightening body that she had lived in and grown used to.

Sofia closed her eyes for the last time. Yusif's body shuddered and tears appeared in his eyes but he did not cry. He didn't look at Narges's eyes, and he avoided Maryam and Nur's gaze as well, as if their eyes' meeting would put a seal on Sofia's death. He sat for some time beside the body, rubbing his gray hair and pulling the shroud across to cover her, then pulling it off again to see her for the last time. He did this five times.

After that, Yusif retreated to his office and sat there alone for two weeks without exchanging a single word with anyone, despite Narges's persistent attempts. After those two weeks, while Narges and Maryam had their breakfast on the veranda they were surprised to see him emerge clean-shaven and wearing new clothes. He sat with them, and without any warning began to talk about his life. He talked about his childhood in this house, his relations with Sofia, about the things he loved and the things he hated. Narges remembered a lot of these things, but she listened as if she was hearing them for the first time. Yusif, it seemed, wanted to defy death by redefining himself.

For a long time Yusif did not go near Sofia's room. He did not the leave the house to visit Kawthar, who sent letters through Nur to which he did not reply. Eventually, however, he went back to his old habits of staying up late in the sleazy hashish dens, and continued his relationship with Kawthar. Narges began a new phase of gloom and almost total withdrawal. She started spending most of her time in front of the television, completely immersed in the film and soap characters, crying profusely at any scene she found the slightest bit moving. She would pick certain characters and unconsciously imitate them. When she saw *Gone with the Wind*, she began to treat herself as if she was Scarlett O'Hara. She didn't continue with this role for long, as she didn't have the energy required to play such a powerful character, especially as she couldn't find anyone to love her as Clark Gable did with Vivien Leigh in the film. It annoyed her to discover that the part of Olivia De Havilland or 'Melanie' suited her better, so she turned to the soaps, always choosing the weakest characters to imitate with her facial expressions, the movements of her hands, and sometimes even with the way she dressed and parted her hair.

The nightingales' song mingles with the chirping of the sparrows and the hooting of a single owl, nesting in a hollow in the trunk of an old mango tree in the rear section of the palace garden. The festive nature of the sound makes passersby feel that the birds have stolen the life from the place's owners.

There was a man called Nasser who they say was pure charisma!

A man named Nasser who would harangue the masses with resounding words, sometimes angrily, sometimes gently. Nasser attracted love, applause, and shouts like a magnet, but he also attracted curses, aggression, and wars. He applauded Nkrumah, Lumumba, and Sukarno, and declared that what had been taken by force could only be recovered by force. He scoffed at what he called imperialism, and the masses carried his image in their hearts, as they shouted, "Abu Khalid, our beloved, tomorrow we shall enter Tel Aviv," and "Gamal, Gamal, we've nationalized the Canal!"

Like a romantic with revolutionary ideas and stillborn dreams, Nasser died and everyone was shattered. Narges wept and hid his picture, stamped with his signature, in the family album, contenting herself with turning him into a story that irritated Maryam. Narges had once sent a passionate letter to Nasser and he had sent her the picture, with "From Abdel Nasser, with regards" written on it. The woman had not been able to cope with her surprise and for weeks would continue to burst into tears whenever she remembered what happened.

When Nasser died, Saleh had already sold his land's harvest of cotton, so he set out for Cairo. Saleh, who was crazy about funeral processions, found the Leader's procession an opportunity not to be missed. He put on his cashmere gallabiya and his black cloak, gripped his splendid ebony stick, and went to the train station. In Cairo he lost himself among the weeping and wailing crowds; he wept with them, cheered, and lost his stick. He stayed for a week in a small hotel on Ramses Square, and returned, loaded with gifts, to tell what he had seen at the great man's funeral. A few years later, with no less eagerness, he had to attend the funeral of another great man, though this time he went in his son's Mercedes, cursing the bastards who murdered good leaders who served the people, made speeches to them day and night, and concluded agreements on their account. Saleh wept, asking God to have mercy on the murdered president, and made a habit of reciting the Fatiha for him and all dead Muslims. He probably nearly died of grief because he would not be attending his private funeral, for funerals to him meant one thing only: lots of stories to bring back and relate to his friends. From his point of view, funerals had their own private philosophy and laws that only he knew. Indeed, during his last years, overcome by illness, he only followed the news of his friends' deaths, so that he could attend their funerals, leaning on his cane. He would drink a cup of coffee when one of them died, then once again give his account of the funeral of the good Leader let down by his incompetent colleagues, and of the faithful Leader who had been treacherously killed.

His love for leaders was a genuine love, free of any self-interest, and it encompassed them all, whatever the differences in their characters and policies. He didn't distinguish between Nasser and Eden, or Kennedy and Sadat. Even Golda Meir, whom he hated, was not exempt from the magic halo that he lovingly put around all our leaders, as if they were above mankind. When he woke at dawn to pray, he always prayed to the president with an attitude of total submission. He repeated this pagan ritual with all four presidents whose terms in office he lived through.

Saleh had begun his working life as a messenger in the British base in Port Said. It was a menial job, but he used to boast about it among his friends, especially as through it he had acquired some English vocabulary, which he would confidently repeat as the others looked at him in amazement. One day he dared to steal some provisions from the base and was sentenced to six months' imprisonment, as a prelude to expulsion from his long-sought paradise. He emerged from prison having made up a story to defend his nationalist credentials, about which there had been some doubt. He claimed to have struck a British officer because he had insulted Egypt and the Egyptians. For this, he claimed, he was punished by being dismissed from his job. Of course, nobody bothered to look closely at the numerous holes in this story of his, and everyone treated him like a hero just because he belonged to their village; especially as, so far as they were concerned, the British were just a vague notion who might as well have been occupying another country. These people knew nothing beyond the borders of their own small village—Cairo and cities like it seemed a long, long way away, even further away than the country of the British.

Saleh lived a good deal of his life believing that the British came from a country bordering Libya. He never understood the secret of the enormous antipathy toward them, just as he could never comprehend why the fedayeen on the canal were fighting and dying. He never began to practice politics in his inimitable way until Nasser came to power, and Saleh began to spout names like Eden, Nehru, Sukarno, and Dayan, without understanding the connection between them. He used to carry around a small brown radio in a cloth bag to listen to news broadcasts and the speeches of the Leader . . . the Leader who had made him a landowner.

Up until then, he had worked as a watchman in El Tagi's vast orchards. He alone knew that the Agricultural Reform Law had not affected El Tagi much, for he had already lost most of his land at the gambling tables, and when the military brought in their laws, they could only confiscate two hundred feddans, which they distributed to the fellaheen — among whom was, of course, Saleh. At this, Saleh felt a pang of conscience, as if he had stolen the land from its owner, so he headed for El Tagi's palace carrying several pounds that he had saved to help him out in the days to come, all wrapped up in a Mahallawi kerchief with brown squares on a faded white background. The young Saleh stepped timidly along the flagstone path with its intricate colors until he reached the steps of the palace. From there, one of the servants led him to where El Tagi was sitting on the terrace savoring the scent of the jasmine plants nearby. Saleh plucked up all his courage and warmly held out his hand with the kerchief containing his money to El Tagi. The man looked at him as if he was mad, before being overcome by his passion for speculation, and inviting Saleh to sit down, with several possibilities going through his mind as to what he might want from him. Saleh sat down on the ground, explaining to the Pasha that the money was payment for the land he had acquired that used to belong to him. At this point, El Tagi burst into a sort of staccato laughter, which seemed as if it would go on forever, and turned his face away. Saleh became totally confused, not knowing how to behave in the face of such an unexpected reaction. El Tagi looked at him with a sarcastic smile, before giving him his splendid ebony stick with the ivory head in the shape of a lion as a way of ending the conversation and reminding him that he was just a servant begging for presents. Saleh didn't understand the message properly because he had never thought of himself as outside the frame of the Pasha's vision. He was simply happy with the ebony stick, the most splendid thing he had seen in his life, and he kept it until he lost it in the crush of the Leader's funeral — the funeral that he was forever giving Maryam a headache with, sitting her on his knees as he told her his never-ending stories, while he left the ash from his cigarettes to fall onto her dresses, making little burn marks that Narges would tell her off about.

For her part, Maryam used to tell him everything about herself, until she grew up and instinct told her to keep her secrets to herself. She didn't tell him, for example, about the dark-skinned boy who could imitate Ricky Martin and smile as seductively as Cary Grant in the old films. The boy who blew her a kiss in the air as she walked along the corridors of her secondary school, and who had dared to touch her hand as he passed by her standing in line in the morning. He had pursued her with his reckless, seductive glances—even though in the end he left her to her fantasies and eloped with Edith.

One evening Edith, this attractive servant of the church—who, despite her father Malak Munir's opposition, had been determined to enter the convent—left everything and disappeared. Rumors then began to circulate about her relationship with the dark-skinned boy who shot pigeons with his rifle, and for some unknown reason, Maryam made herself bear responsibility for what had happened. She couldn't face Amm Malak or Tante Helena, who continued to howl and scream and put earth over her head for a whole week. Helena accepted condolences for the loss of her daughter, and for a long time afterwards wore black, for thanks to her daughter she had drunk from the cup of what she regarded as a double disgrace—first, her daughter had eloped with a man, and second, this man belonged to a different religion.

Malak was always making fun of his daughter, whom he nicknamed 'Shaykha.' He would watch her as she arranged the jars of bees' honey or prized the honeycombs from their wooden frames, amazed by her excessive silence and self-absorption. He became almost frantic when he saw that she had a completely different personality with her friends, especially Maryam.

For a long time he had had an aversion to his daughter's repeated visits to El Tagi's palace; despite that he would question her with a childlike infatuation about what she had seen there. There was a double wall surrounding the palace, formed by a stone wall and another wall of tall gazorina trees that aroused his curiosity in an almost irrational way about what there might be inside this terrifying house.

But the thing that most piqued his interest was the garden surrounding the palace, the area of which alone was more than two feddans. He asked Edith for the most precise details of the trees and flowers planted there.

One of his daydreams was to turn this garden into a meadow for the beehives that he kept. He believed that honey from hives like these would taste better than any other sort. Edith would listen to him without knowing how to reply. She would simply let out an involuntary laugh, as she saw in her mind's eye enormous swarms of unruly bees chasing Maryam, her mother and father, and everyone in the palace who annoyed her whenever she trod its paths.

I t is said that an angel in the form of a hoopoe used to pick its food from the palace fruits. It would fly off carrying the choicest peaches or plums in its beak before alighting onto some empty spot. It would peck gently at the fruit, then abandon it; and if anyone ate the fruit that had been pecked, he would immediately go mad.

Maryam walked along the streets of the city like a woman in a trance, not knowing whether or not she was in the real world. Everything had become distant from her, so distant and remote that it was frightening. The people who had been part of her life had changed into mere ghosts, visiting her from time to time, then suddenly leaving her, abandoning her without the slightest sympathy to whirlpools of anxiety and madness.

Maryam walked almost unconsciously, clutching her clothes firmly to her body and pounding the pavements with her feet. She forced herself to utter a few meaningless words, just to persuade herself that she still existed. She was still in the world that had been eager to expel her from her first moment in it. She had been a sickly child, more dead than alive, whose stomach rejected everything that was put into it through constant vomiting or diarrhea. Narges had been forced to give her enormous doses of glucose so that the life would not escape from her cells. Recently, Maryam had begun to relive the taste of that liquid in her mouth, conscious of it in every drink and piece of food that she swallowed, as if it were the only thing she had tasted during her past life; a life that had now turned into tiny pieces that made no sense beside each other, and of which nothing remained except this acrid taste.

She had chosen to live alone, far from everyone she knew, but how was it that she had actually made this choice? Could a family like hers leave its daughter to live alone without even asking after her or visiting her? Where was this family, then? Why could she find no trace of them when she visited the village that was supposed to be hers? No one knew her there and she knew no one. She walked like a ghost . . . lightly, ethereally even . . . borne on the gentle breeze that rocked the place. She had searched every inch of the village for the Tiger, for Narges, Kawthar, and Saleh, for traces of Yusif and Sofia, but to no avail. Even El Tagi's palace did not exist. The tombs that she knew well, that until the last moment she had thought contained her loved ones, were not the same. Everything was different from the way she had imagined it—quite frighteningly so. Maryam felt that she was confronting death. A new Adam had set sail on the raging sea of existence after his God had abandoned him.

She sat down in a pathway between two rows of facing graves and leaned back against one of them. She lit a cigarette with a shaking hand and started to smoke, hoping to calm down a little. The smell of mint and basil reminded her of Sofia. She smiled unintentionally as she visualized Sofia on her endless wanderings, carrying her dirty scraps of paper and the twigs of mint and basil, followed by the violent clatter of her footsteps and the heavy smell of the sticky juice from the succulents that stained her hands and clothes. Where was she now? Was she simply lying in some dark pit, or were there other graves in heaven weighed down by the lethargy facing her? Were there paths full of dirty scraps of paper for her to gather with no rebuke from anyone, in a place where certainly nothing and no one would be like her? Maryam had become certain that everything she relied on was futile, but she no longer knew who these people were who pursued her wherever she went, asking her to come back to join them and acknowledge them. She wished it could all just be a long nightmare that would end when she woke up yawning in a warm bed to tell her relatives the complicated details of her dreams. Yahya passed through her mind and she asked him not to leave her alone and exposed to all these questions, but to come back so that she would have him for company. But she knew that he was on their side. Her destiny was linked to theirs. Their existence meant his existence, and their disappearance meant that he too had never been there. She started up, shook the dust off her clothes and straightened her hair with her hand. Slowly she walked out of the place.

The objects and memories that seem to be receding as they fade further and further into the background are not really far away. On the contrary, they penetrate inside us as they are absorbed by our blood, mingling with every atom to such an extent that they succeed in deceiving us. They make us think that our memory has completely wiped them out, until we are surprised when they suddenly burst forth like scattered fragments, to form a total state with no clear details . . . a state that moves us to sadness or nostalgia, or to exhilaration whose source we can never fathom.

Thus the smell of mint and sweet basil could bring back memories of Sofia as she was in the flesh, a cloud of smoke could recall Yusif, a frown etched on the features of a face could instantly encapsulate every detail of Narges, and a funeral marquee could call to mind Saleh's peaceable spirit.

But what could Maryam leave behind her after she died? What would remain of her in the consciousness of two or three people at most?

Maryam moved in a city of cardboard. Nothing but buildings and streets of paper, waiting for some ill-natured breeze to remove them from existence, exposing the ruin that had taken hold of their essence.

It was a hideous woodworm eating away at everything. A sly woodworm that burrowed away slowly, so slowly that no one noticed as it worked relentlessly, piercing the very heart of things.

The city was wrapped in a gentle darkness in which Maryam moved without being conscious of anything around her. Her mind was working furiously, even though she was unable to understand. She was not merely preoccupied at that moment with Yahya's disappearance or with what had happened to Radwa. She was searching for something deeper: for the person who had driven everyone into the whirlpool of madness. Had Sofia gone mad and everything else followed? Or was madness the root and everything else mere delusion?

Yahya had taken her forcibly into his world. He had stripped her of everything she was tied to; he wanted to possess her soul.

He had dragged her with him toward things she regarded as more or less capital offences. With him, she had not stopped for a moment to consider what was happening. She had been unaware of any of the constraining factors, so that when she tried to retrieve their relationship, she felt that they were moving in a deadening void. The first day at his house, she began to move like a woman in a trance. She would feel things gently. She would move around from the kitchen to the lounge to his study, knocking against the furniture as he watched her in amazement.

But the sense that had taken hold of her, and that she was heroically trying to overcome, was that the smell of death inhabited Yahya. It both emanated from him and surrounded him, creating an obscure aura. She was breathing death in her life with him in a way that she never understood.

Vague, disordered, and disconnected memories were all that bound her to him now. Sometimes a multitude of details rushed into her mind, clear and complete scenes, but she could never work out whether these scenes and events had actually happened or not. His childish smile and crafty look overflowed in her memory, but time and again she would wonder: if this person had existed, where has he gone?

Yesterday while she was rummaging through the papers stuffed into Sofia's wooden box in the Abdin flat, she found a certificate relating to the marriage of Maryam Yusif el Tagi and Yahya el Gindi. The photograph on the certificate bore the same features that her face did now: a bronze complexion, jet black hair that covered her shoulders, and black eyes. It was completely different from the Maryam she had known, with long brown hair, a fine nose, and wandering, honey-colored eyes inherited from Sofia. As for Yahya, his photograph was exactly as she remembered him. But what really made her pause was the existence of a marriage certificate .... She was certain, or she had been, that she had never been married to Yahya, and that there should never have been a certificate.

At the beginning of her relationship with him, Maryam had dreamed that she was sleeping naked in his arms, that he was also naked, and that as he embraced her tightly, the door opened and through it came Yusif, Narges, Kawthar, Saleh, Zaynab, and some strange children calling out her name. "Shame, shame!" she shouted, and began to repeat the word in a melodramatic way as she tried to cover her body. Maryam felt that this dream was simultaneously continuing to dominate her relationship with Yahya and to expose it.

When she was with him there was someone watching her and mocking her desperate attempts to engage with life. Was he really a journalist at that newspaper? Why had she found no trace of him there? How had she met him? How had their acquaintance consolidated itself? Maryam did not know how to answer these questions. She had to adapt to the state of bewilderment in which she was living, to rely only on the things that she could be certain of.

Yahya's house was not large, and the whole area was carefully controlled, with nothing left to the imagination. There were not many spaces in it, for Yahya had been careful to fill the whole space with furniture—as if pieces of furniture could act like pegs that would fasten the place down, and stop it from flying away and dispersing in the air. The walls were over-flowing with pictures and photographs. Sometimes Maryam imagined that there was a small child sharing their life but she could never recall anything about the child except for its blond hair and honey-brown eyes. Was it her son? But she had never experienced pregnancy or childbirth. If she had, it would have been etched inside her . . . and then again, her body carried no trace of this experience.

Who was this child, then? Did he belong to Yahya alone? Ever since her life had so suddenly changed and she had become exposed to these questions, Maryam had sensed that the key to the puzzle of her life lay first with Yahya and second with Radwa. Their sudden disappearance into thin air was killing her. Was there a conspiracy linking the two of them together?

More than once she tried to reach Yahya's house but it led to nothing. Her information suggested that he was living on a particular street in Manyal, but when she made her way to this street and the building in which the flat was supposed to be, she was surprised to find herself in front of a quite different building that she had never known or even walked past. She got a grip on her impetuosity and asked the watchman for Yahya's flat, but the man just looked at her contemptuously and cursed uncouth young women as if Maryam had committed a crime. She went away, dragging her feet with difficulty. She was on the point of losing consciousness. The streets had turned into wicked creatures in her eyes, conspiring against her and surrendering her to a terrifying game of repetition. They had become completely alike, like vast mazes put together by a well-trained hand for Maryam to lose herself in. She had started to feel afraid of walking in the shadowy lanes of this city with its meager light, on which the street lamps apparently had no effect.

In the past, Maryam knew the streets of the city by heart. She liked to hang around in them. She had looked with affection at the dirt piling up on the buildings and trees and at the exhaust fumes weaving their cloaks in the air. She even knew the places where particular beggars congregated. But she was now confronted by a different, hellish city that was trying to expel her from the universe. She knew none of the people who lived there. It was as if they had all been replaced by different creatures trying desperately to imitate them so that the game would not be discovered and everyone could remain in his own private maze. Otherwise, how was it that Maryam no longer recognized any of her once favorite places? How was it that everyone she had known had disappeared and left her in this void?

'Problem woman' was the name that Yahya had given her. How was it that they had now exchanged roles, so that he had become a mercurial being who slipped through her fingers? He used to insist that she would inevitably destroy him, but she could not now remember whether he had been serious in this belief or whether he had been joking. For her part, she felt that he was bringing her closer to death by making her feel that he was a close friend she could live with. She had often blamed herself for this feeling that she had toward him but the matter was outside of her control, for despite his obvious vitality and zest for life, his body gave out the smell of death, which Maryam's nose never failed to detect. Unlike Yusif, Yahya had loved life and faced it head on. With his whole being, he had tried to push Maryam on the same road. He knew that she came from a family of the dead who had become only hazy memories that gave nothing away about the people behind them. They had turned into mere metaphors: the smell of mint and sweet basil, a funeral marquee, a frown etched on a face, and a cloud of cigarette smoke reinforced by hashish.

Maryam wanted to be philosophical about death and had fallen into its cunningly set snares. She had convinced herself that the smell came from Yahya and never stopped to ask herself whether it might come from her. Yahya's childlike eyes had brought her closer to her destined fate. The twenty years' difference in age between them had been enough to weave a web of seductive stories to which Maryam listened shaking with emotion, putting out of her mind the fact that Yahya was nothing but a synonym for the death that was settling over her life.

Maryam now started to wander a lot around the streets in the city center, which spread out like the tentacles of an octopus. She would dawdle for a long time in front of the places she had known with him, looking at the faces of the customers through the outer glass but hardly recognizing any of them, despite the fact that she had never left these places. She continued to wander about endlessly. When she walked down Kasr el Nil Street at night, however, from the intersection with Sharif Street she was overcome by fear. Maryam felt that all her fear of the new city was justified, because this part of Kasr el Nil Street, dark and deserted, with its old buildings that looked like frightening, mythical animals, seemed to have come straight out of a horror story.

Apricot trees were the only trees that did not grow well in the palace garden. The small trees would grow until they reached a certain stage, then stop. They would not flower, but would remain just as they were, slender stumps laden with dark green leaves, with no branches growing off them.

Maryam had been used to being in first place among her schoolmates right up to secondary school. Her superiority was evident to all. She loved chemistry, physics, and math. Her favorite hobby was to sit for hours at her desk solving problems of mechanics, trigonometry, and differential and integral calculus, seeking out the trickiest problems in physics in order to crack their secrets, or putting together made-up chemical formulas in which she mixed all sorts of elements and substances.

Her chemistry teacher told her that life was nothing but chemistry, that love was the same, and so were the air we breathed and the food we ate. Maryam laughed at the time, but inside herself she believed what he said.

She would sit for a long time in her room listening to Radio Monte Carlo, to the Magic Worlds of Fayiz Muqaddasi and the seductive voices of Antoine Barud and Habib Hammoud, turning the people around her into equations that she consistently failed to solve.

She knew that chlorine plus sodium gave us sodium chloride and that hydrogen plus oxygen produced water but she didn't know what Yusif and Narges made. She didn't understand which of their constituent elements prevented interaction between them. She imagined everyone in El Tagi's palace as elements incapable of interaction with their surroundings—as catalysts, like manganese dioxide, that facilitate a reaction but do not react themselves. Solitary beings, destined to remain like that: Sofia chasing her papers, Narges living with her imaginary ghosts, and Yusif with his solitude. El Tagi too had remained a prisoner, sitting endlessly on the terrace surrounded by jasmine bushes on every side—the same bushes that had given him a chest allergy and led to his death, strangled by their sweet fragrance.

The complex questions that Maryam busied herself solving were, together with the old films of James Dean and Yves Montand, the reason that she paid no attention to her other subjects. She consequently failed to gain enough marks to qualify her to enroll in the Faculty of Medicine or Pharmacy as Narges wanted her to. Maryam betrayed herself when she refused to enroll in the Faculty of Science and decided to study philosophy. She plunged headlong into the study of existentialism and logical positivism. She compared Hegel, Marx, and Nietzsche, structuralism and deconstructionism, while the laws of mathematics evaporated from her memory. They had become no more than obscure symbols with no precise significance.

At first, Maryam paid no attention to this and dedicated herself to her new world, persuading herself that she would find her true self there. But later she suddenly started to feel depressed. She felt that she was about to fall into a bottomless pit when she read or heard terms like 'The Archimedes

Principle,' 'Newton's Laws' or 'Pythagoras's Theorem.' How could her memory be letting her down like this? Where had these things gone? Why did she feel that her mind had become empty . . . just a useless cavity?

There was a terrifying void centered on her brain, a void that enjoyed an amazing power of attraction, sucking information and ideas into itself, only for the memory to rid itself of them by expelling them. Maryam was afraid of this void, whose power seemed to be forever increasing, to the point where it would succeed in erasing all the information she had learned since she had become conscious of life, then hand it over to someone else, or else leave it to blow away in midair like the papers Sofia had collected one stormy morning. Her foot had slipped and she had fallen to the ground, and immediately the scraps of paper blew away, oblivious to the old woman's shrieks. Could the papers that Sofia collected from the streets and rubbish heaps be a substitute intellect and memory—a substitute for her own intellect and memory that were being eaten away by decay?

When the philosophical ideas and theories also began to contract in Maryam's memory, she found herself confronted by a terrifying possibility: the possibility that she might be on the way to her grandmother's fate. She didn't surrender to this nightmare but began to read avidly about the subjects that had disappeared from her mind, whether scientific or philosophical. It was as if she was meeting those ideas and theories for the first time. She made a great effort to understand them, but the understanding only lasted for a few moments, after which everything turned into utterly obscure headings.

The dream that kept her awake more than any other was one in which she suddenly found herself faced with having to pass the General Secondary Examination in mathematics. The year was about to end and she had not even looked at the syllabus, and knew nothing about the laws of mathematics or methods for solving equations. The details of the dream, which repeated itself endlessly, impressed themselves on her so intensely that she practically choked, but when she woke up the sensation ended suddenly. For several minutes, however, she remained unconvinced that she wasn't obliged to pass the exam.

To this dream was added another dream, in which she found herself naked in the midst of a crowd of people, trying desperately but without success to cover herself. This was the dream that Yahya had explained to her as meaning that she had gone mad.

From time to time Maryam used to ruminate on these two dreams—together, later, with the dream about her death—savoring the vague discomfort that the three dreams left inside her. She delighted in the recollection of the smallest, most disturbing details, as if by doing so she would be drawn closer to the world that had slipped through her fingers without her noticing. As though she could be returned to the place she had so often clung to but which she also feared—to Zaynab, Sofia, and Yusif, but above all to Narges, and even the Tiger.

When Zaynab invited her to her house, she would walk fearfully through the garden with its intertwined branches that separated the house from the palace. She would climb the four steps to find herself on the wide veranda ringed with jasmine bushes. As usual, the door would be ajar. One of these visits was implanted in her memory and refused to leave it. The house was almost completely in darkness. Maryam stepped trembling into the enormous hall, heading toward the bubbling of Zaynab's shisha as she sat on her own private sofa at the rear of the hall facing the door. Maryam whispered her name, and Zaynab stretched out her hand and pulled her down to sit beside her.

The blinds on the window had been blown open by the strong breeze outside, so that a glimmer of light filtered in, allowing the girl to see Zaynab with her stern expression and bright eyes. Her gray hair was raised up and she was wearing a wine-colored Moroccan gown covered with small circles of gold embroidery, with larger circles on the chest and different patterns around the sleeves. Her voice was deeper than usual and her words were disjointed, with no clear meaning. She was asking Maryam about things to do with her studies and whether anyone was annoying her in school, or things of that sort. It was an ordinary conversation, dominated by the gurgling of the shisha and by Zaynab's voice, which had turned into a sort of hiss. Maryam answered her impatiently, her mind wandering elsewhere, somewhere that she could not quite identify. It was a locality overflowing with blood, with the smells of henna, jasmine, basil and mint, and the glow of mantle lamps.

It was when El Tagi died. Zaynab had presided over the funeral arrangements herself. Instead of earth or sand, she had spread five large sacks of soft henna on the floor of the tomb and had smeared the door with her hands full of clay mixed with straw. She had set up a small tent in the passage between his tomb and the row of tombs opposite and stayed in the tent night and day with the help of the mantle lamp, attended by a number of her servants for a period of three months for fear that someone might steal El Tagi's body and mutilate it. Until this day, Zaynab had gone herself to water the basil, mint, and succulents that she had planted there with her own hands.

Maryam had listened to that story many times but had never understood why anyone should want to mutilate the body of her grandfather. There were many things that she did not know.

There was an old story, apparently, of a strange blood feud that started as a result of some financial arguments between El Tagi and a family from a neighboring village. It was also said that Zaynab had had a twenty-year old son, and that a member of a rival family had murdered this son to take revenge on El Tagi. Zaynab had then paid a hired killer, 'the Tiger,' who had killed the murderer and dismembered his corpse. He was even said to have taken his liver and a glass of his blood to Zaynab, who had grilled the liver and fed it to her servants.

This terrible vengeance attributed to Zaynab contributed to the awe that everyone felt toward her—in contrast to Sofia, whom they had treated from the beginning with indifference, perhaps because she was so aloof and wrapped up in herself, as if she was living in a different universe.

When El Tagi died, Sofia hadn't attended the funeral procession or the funeral rites. As soon as she heard the wailing from Zaynab's house and saw the servants passing on the news in a state of confusion, she had packed her bag and ordered the driver to take her to her flat in Cairo, to the consternation of everyone in the palace. The air had already been heavy with scattered whisperings of the strange madness that had afflicted her, but these whisperings had now, by her own actions, become a tangible fact.

She stayed in her flat for two whole months. When she came back, no one attempted to exchange a single word with her. She restyled her gray hair as it had been two decades earlier and left it hanging down over her shoulders. She started to walk around the palace, her voice echoing the songs of Layla Murad and Ragaa Abduh. When Yusif approached her, she carried on in her bemused state and behaved as if she didn't know him.

It seemed that she was unable to come to terms with the man's death. In her eyes, it was as though he had disappeared but not died, perhaps because she had never seen his corpse or seen him as they were laying him to rest.

Sofia lived in this insane state for a considerable period, waiting for the man to reappear from the dead. When she woke from this madness, she became immersed in another spell that was just as voracious. She started screaming during the night, cursing Zaynab and accusing her of killing El Tagi in conspiracy with the Tiger, whom she described as Zaynab's lover. Silence was no longer an option in the face of these accusations, so Yusif shut her up in an out-of-the-way room.

When Maryam opened her eyes on life, the room was known as Sofia's room. By this time, however, Sofia's madness had moved on to a new stage. She had begun to go out at six o'clock every morning carrying a plastic bag to hold the dirty papers she collected from the streets and piles of rubbish. She would wander in the streets until she reached the cemeteries. Completely exhausted, she would sink to the ground in front of one of them at random, before returning with some sprigs of basil and mint that she had picked there, her hands stained with the sticky, bitter juice of succulents.

Sofia diligently undertook that ritual pilgrimage until the last day of her life. Yusif never succeeded in persuading her to abandon it. Only when she returned to the palace would Narges occasionally plant a needle in her vein, with an injection of tranquilizers to prevent her body becoming worn out from the endless hysterical motions.

That was the woman Maryam knew by the name of Sofia. She had never seen the beautiful Sofia, the daughter of the Albanian cloth merchant, named by her mother after a Greek friend she had grown up with among the diverse religions and nationalities in the El Daher quarter. Nor had she known the young wife who had moved in to live with Ahmed el Tagi in his palace that nestled in that secluded spot. The image that appeared before her—of an old woman with straggly hair and wandering eyes—was completely at odds with the subject's earlier life. Had she reached a point where she was contradicting her true nature, or was it rather that she had now arrived at her true nature, stripped by time of its accumulated wrappings and counterfeit shells? It seemed to her that all her life she had been struggling, only to end up as this flimsy creature, constantly shaking, forever wandering about in search of scattered papers, as if collecting them could return the universe to its former course.

Only one thing would restore Sofia to reality—meeting the Tiger during her endless wanderings. She would shake as she laid into him with a never-ending stream of abuse in a voice worn out by the years. The man would hurry off without paying her any attention, taking refuge in the solitude that he had maintained since he first set foot in the village. Even now, no one knew his real name. They had nicknamed him 'the Tiger' since he was obviously vicious and because he always wore a commando camouflage suit. But all the information anyone had on him was pure speculation, for he never talked about himself at all. He lived in a small house far from civilization, surrounded by a fence made of dry canes. People passing the house would catch a glimpse from a distance of some palm prints in blood on the shabby wooden door, but they soon moved on when the three fierce dogs that constantly circled the house appeared, barking like rabid animals as soon as anyone approached the cane fence.

The Tiger had a peculiar way of walking that made people around him feel that an enormous tank was making the earth shake beneath them. He would walk along with a pile of newspapers under his arm. The newspapers were a simple cover for the fact that he was selling drugs—hashish and opium, to be precise, for the man despised bango and other newfangled varieties, which he considered fit only for youths new to the habit.

The Tiger would usually set down his load under an ancient sycamore tree, opposite an old café on the asphalt road that ran through the village from the west. He would stay sitting beside the spread of newspapers until sunset, then gather up those that he still had with him and leave them with the old café owner, cursing him with a few coarse expressions as a sort of joke. He would also slip copies of old papers between the new ones and sell them to customers as today's papers. If anyone dared to look at the date at the top of the page, the Tiger would rant and rave until the customer shut up and went off dragging his steps.

Maryam had had no contact with the Tiger until Yusif started taking her with him to the cafés and drug dens that he frequented. A strange relationship established itself between the two men. Despite their differences of personality and environment, they were bound together by a familiarity that defied comprehension. The Tiger was of course the source of hashish and opium for Yusif with the amputated arm and fickle temperament, but everyone always seemed to think that the relationship went beyond that.

Later, during the nights that Maryam was sure she had spent in the hostel, the image of the Tiger with his white, disheveled beard, narrow eyes and dark yellow teeth, hounded her for reasons that she did not know. She saw him in her dreams as an enormous phantom pursuing her with blood-spattered hands, while in front of him crouched the corpses of El Tagi, Zaynab, Sofia, and Yusif, all drowning in their own blood. The Tiger would put his hands in the blood and smear it on Maryam's body, leaving the indelible marks of bloody hands side by side staining her skin. She would give herself up to a loud wailing that turned into hysterical laughter before the Tiger's body and soul took possession of her and she disappeared completely, seeing herself with the man's features, hoarse voice, and history stained with blood.

They say that there is a room fragrant with the scent of jasmine, a second room thick with the smell of wild roses, and other rooms from which waft the scents of lemon flowers, orange blossom, or ambergris. Until we reach fifty rooms with fifty different bouquets.

The smells mingle sensuously in the halls and corridors, making yet more new fragrances to captivate the heart.

It's a life of glass, a brittle life that can be smashed at any moment, by any chance event. And her particular life, if she has a life, is glassy twice over. Everything around her is clear glass that cannot hide what is behind it. There are no surprises, no secrets, nothing. Despite that, she finds herself lost in mazes so cunningly constructed that it is difficult to escape.

She looks at them and knows what is going on in their minds. She sees them, though they do not see her. She is immersed in their petty details as she waits for the moment of escape that has become so distant that it frightens her. Far off, even though it is nearer to her than she had imagined.

Ever since she won the right to live away from Maryam's worn-out body, she had not been as happy as she had anticipated. On the contrary, her fears had begun to encircle her so that they almost annihilated her.

She had never known death before, and had therefore never trained herself to confront it. Now, she had become weak before it . . . surrendering to it completely, trembling at the sight of a tree's leaves suddenly quivering if the meowing of a cat became louder than was normal. Sometimes she wondered how all this could be happening, even though she had lived with the most hideous sounds and the foulest smells.

Could life, despite its fragility, be as heavy and frightening as this? This was the first question that crossed her mind when she detached herself from Maryam, before that moment that seems so faraway to her now. A terrible cloud was encircling them both, a cloud like a frame encircling their lives, making them so hazy that neither of them was aware what exactly had happened. She can remember nothing about it, nothing except for the dark mist and some feeble rays of light that were trying unsuccessfully to penetrate it, thereby confirming the smog rather than dispersing it.

At first, there had been a vehicle that she thought she found herself inside. This vehicle was making its way with difficulty through water, as rain showers collected on the windscreen, turning into intersecting streams that the wipers could not disperse.

She turned her gaze away from the rivulets of water. Her eyes met the driver's eyes. She thought he had the appearance of a madman. She quickly looked away and again concentrated her attention on the flows of rain slipping down the car's windscreen. The man was driving with one hand and moving his other hand around nervously, searching for something or other in the car's glove box. Then he would suddenly stop searching, and put his hand over his mouth or press it hard on his forehead.

A few seconds later, her body started to tremble strangely. From time to time he looked at her with a fiery glance in the mirror. She was terrified by the possibility that the man might be deranged or under the influence of a powerful drug. She suddenly discovered that real terror did not lie in exposure to the danger of a lethal enemy with a dead heart, but rather in falling into the clutches of an adversary who cannot control himself. To lose one's mind is a terrifying thing, even if we have up to then been unaware of the mind's existence.

She woke from her thoughts to an even heavier downpour and pained mutterings from the driver. She had asked him to slow down but he told her that the matter was completely outside his control. His expression in the mirror appeared to be a plea for help. This made her fall apart completely, for despite her fear during the last few moments that he might attack her, a part of her felt reassured by the power and stability that she assumed he possessed. It was like the simplistic guesses we make about kidnappers.

She had been thinking that anything he might do would be safer than the character who had bared its teeth. The driver's cry for help shattered her last hope, and awakened her to the fact that he was also not in control. They were both at the mercy of unknown forces.

She saw thick beads of sweat gathering on his face while he cursed and swore, looking uneasily at the road lined with thick trees on both sides. The road was becoming so narrow that it was difficult for the car to pass. She began to shiver violently. Before she completely lost consciousness, she imagined that a giant hand had thrown her half-conscious body out of the car, where it rolled several times in a jungle-like garden. Sharp thorns scratched her face and body. She felt fresh blood pouring from her body in several places. She began to regain consciousness again. A dog was barking nearby in an injured tone. Black creatures like cats were running beside her, knocking against her body. She heard an indistinct mumbling from a nearby villa. She pulled herself together and made for the four steps that led into the place. She pushed at the half open door and entered timidly, unaccustomed to her limping steps. Everything in here was different from the environment outside. In the middle of the room stood an ancient heater in which a fire was blazing, surrounded by pinkish colored bricks. Beside it a rocking chair was still slowly rocking, as if someone had just left. An ancient sofa and some old style armchairs were scattered here and there. The walls were entirely covered with gleaming mirrors, on which were reflected the heater and its flames, the armchairs and the rocking chair, and everything in the room except Maryam. She could find no trace of her own body on the surfaces of those cursed mirrors. She let out a crazed scream of desperation.

She never knew who moved her, so that she found herself in the morning half awake, half asleep in a warm bed. All the rules had been suspended. Nothing was as she had known it—everything was absolutely different. The room was bathed in a blazing red light, and the pieces of furniture were in illogical places. The door was open onto a large room that looked narrower than it really was, and through it could be seen the Venetian blinds on the balcony door flapping vigorously. Only the chandelier seemed to be challenging her with its obscene face. Fixed to the ceiling and shaped like a tree branch with three leaves each holding a lamp, it gradually moved closer to her until it nearly collided with her face, before suddenly lifting itself up to return to the attack.

Voices crowded her on all sides. The voices seemed to have no need for the people they belonged to, but merged to form a single sound that moved independently, as if to demonstrate how fragile the body was. As she woke up, she renewed her acquaintance with life, and recovered from the oppressive shaking fit. It annoyed her that she would never know whether what she had experienced was a dream or something else.

She tried to forget the whole thing. But the eyes of the driver continued to press her insistently. She opened the door to the balcony and looked at the sky outside. She saw the sun shining. The streets were clean and dry, as if they had not been touched by rain for some time. The half-deserted villa nestled opposite the balcony, completely given up to the silence. Unlike the neighboring houses, it was completely at ease with silence and darkness: there were no night lights, no voices, and no arguments emerging from it . . . nothing at all.

It seemed to her to belong to her old world. She used to watch it during the evening to reassure herself about the dreadful silence that had engulfed it. Every evening between six and seven o'clock a thin woman with a squint would appear as if she were looking for something on the veranda. She would walk up and down several times before sitting down on a bamboo chair with crisscross patterned cushions. She would rest her elbows on the round table and stay sitting for some time, her eyes fixed on the entrance to the little garden that was like a miniature forest in need of someone to tidy it. Then she would quickly retreat inside the villa with hurried, bewildered steps.

With her clothes and hairstyle, the woman looked like someone who had stepped out of a picture book from the 1950s.

Her face was almost devoid of expression and her squinting look had surrendered to depression.

When Maryam looked at her, the other woman wondered whether her eyes saw the world exactly as Maryam did. Did people in general, she wondered, see things around them in the same way as others? What if there were very slight differences from one person to another, which when added together might lead to alarming results, as alarming as the chasm that separated their world from hers? Was it sight that defined everything? They existed because she could see them, while she did not exist because she was outside their field of vision.

What if this woman was just a figment of the imagination? Why didn't she call to her out loud? Then perhaps she would give some indication that she was there.

At this point, though, she always stopped and did not try to go on with her tiresome musings. She was hemmed in by the stern features and glassy look of a woman of around fifty, unconcerned with anything but what was inside her, cocooned in her fantasies.

She tried to imitate real life. She would arrange the place, clean the plastic flowers of the dust that had accumulated on them, and check that the pieces of furniture were in exactly the right places. From time to time she would amuse herself by watching time disintegrate before her eyes into infinitely small fragments that were difficult to piece together again—though when they decided that they should be linked up, they would press her between their jagged edges. She would observe time that heeded no one, but rather wandered in a daze with complete indifference, shattering everything into tiny splinters that resembled it and like time turned into dust scattered in the air. In her imagination, she guessed that it must be a very lonely, melancholy person, looking for others like itself, but unable to relate to them except by swallowing them up in its vast belly.

She doesn't remember now when she came up against the squinting look for the first time, but it was an exceptional moment in her new life. It seemed like an obscure message in need of decoding. The droop in one of the woman's eyes seemed to be pointing to some dreadful malady that had afflicted the soul of the universe.

The thin woman was busy doing something on her balcony when a strangled cry escaped from inside. She started up and threw a quick glance at the other woman before turning toward the noise.

Her startled movement aroused the curiosity of the other woman. She woke early the next day and crept out to examine the rubbish bags in front of the villa but she didn't find anything out of the ordinary in them. Just some cotton bandages with blood on them, glass medicine bottles with the necks pulled off, and spots of dry blood covering everything.

There were no remains of food, empty juice bottles, or even fruit peelings, and if it weren't for the woman with the squint and the moaning sound that had begun to get louder, she would have been convinced that the house was completely deserted.

She was drawn toward the moaning which was becoming louder still. To her surprise, she found the door open. She found herself in the hall with the ancient heater, the rocking chair, and the scattered armchairs, but this time the mirrors seemed completely solid. They did not reflect any of these things. She stepped into the hallway where the moaning was coming from and opened the door to the room.

She saw the thin woman lying beside the body of an old man who looked like El Tagi, with her hand on his breast. A thick thread of dark blood trickled onto the floor in the direction of the door. She walked forward slowly and was caught off guard by her reflection in a small mirror beside the bed. She started to shake. Her eyes were fixed on the squinting look and slender body that challenged her crossly before being plunged into thick darkness.

After she regained consciousness she did not leave the villa. She settled there and never again saw the place from which she used to watch it. She would set out on her wanderings, eager to get to grips with every aspect of life, and would return on her own accord to the deserted villa. Whenever she looked in a mirror, she would be confronted by the slender body and squinting look.

It might have been supposed that she would assume the features of Maryam, her honey-colored eyes, her brown hair, and her fine nose. Most of all, she coveted her strong presence and the proud, aristocratic manner that she had inherited from her Albanian grandmother.

But she didn't know what devil had cast her into this thin body and given her these stern features.

What hell was this? She knew all their feelings and all the details of their lives, but she didn't possess them, didn't feel them and didn't even understand them. Who was responsible for what had happened?

Had she misjudged Maryam's spiritual strength and thus been unable to weaken her all those years, or shake her trust in the world in which she moved? She knew her thoughts before they came into her mind. She was Maryam, and Maryam was she, and now, after her act for which she would be cursed forever, one of them had parted from the other. She no longer knew Maryam's fate. Had her body collapsed after she had left it? Had she kept her body and her looks as they were? Or had she never been in Maryam's body at all, but had just been tailing it like a shadow, an unseen ghost that followed her and competed with her for the space she occupied? Her destiny required that she should not make Maryam aware of her, but should leave her at center stage. Even if she harmed Maryam, she had to carry on in such a way that it would seem as if Maryam had harmed herself: a silly girl putting herself into dangerous situations, or a poor girl plagued by bad luck, that is how it had to look.

But she had rebelled against her destiny. Maryam was a brilliant child, so brilliant that she couldn't stand her. Whenever she saw her untroubled gaze, she lay awake in agony. Why couldn't she have been born like that, with a mother and father and family, even if it was a family like El Tagi's with a history full of holes and gaps and ugly secrets?

How extraordinary that someone like Maryam should be split between admiration for Kawthar, who paid no attention to the gossip that surrounded her, and Narges, who was in love with Greta Garbo, Greer Garson, and the stars of the black-and-white movies, and who flitted between their personalities without really living out her own.

She was not fond of the human lifestyle and had no romantic ambition to experience human emotions. Indeed, it went further than that. They enjoyed better conditions of life than she or others like her did. Her abilities exceeded theirs many times over, but despite that, they monopolized everything, leaving her nothing but crumbs, and went off consumed by their ignorance and self-importance and taking no notice of her existence, crushing her under their boots as they walked. Dancing or arguing, it was all one.

She knew that no one would believe her and that her attempts to establish her own identity would be just a game in space. Perhaps it was because Maryam had preceded her into corporeal existence in this world, or perhaps it was because they had both found themselves together in the maze without the slightest degree of certainty. At all events, whichever one of them first had enough proof to corroborate the justice and correctness of her position could expel the other from this narrow realm in which nearly everyone chokes to death but which all make desperate efforts to preserve.

She existed before Maryam existed, but her existence was dependent on Maryam's existence, and her life remained a mere echo of Maryam's choices. She tried to recall the smells, sights, and sounds imprinted on her self, to disentangle the lives they had led together in preparation for reconstituting herself again. A life that would embrace her alone, far from the conceits of Maryam and all those with her, or at least a life that would include the two of them as equal partners together.

It was always smells that came to her first and that she remembered most strongly: the smell of the putrid waters of the Nile in the early morning; the strong smell of coffee beans coming from Zaynab's house; the penetrating smell of tobacco clinging to Yusif's skin and breath; the smell of sawdust at the bottom of the palace garden; and the smells of mint, basil, jasmine, and food mingling.

A multitude of smells imprinted on her life and gently enveloping it, smells separated one from another by images, memories, events, and people, rather than the other way around.

Her history had been formed by collisions, blows, and wounds. There was no romance about it; it was the simple truth. At first, they had been rough and extremely violent collisions in a dark world whose horizons were jet black. She had learned that the hardest and most painful blows were those whose origin you did not know, which your eyes could not follow as they came toward you. They just surprised you with a lethal impact. She spent a considerable time in that world of darkness waiting for the moment of her release. Hideous screams and terrifying cries of pain from those waiting for the time of release had already shrilled in her ears. Thousands of times she had fallen into bottomless wells. Her soul had been shattered into a thousand splinters. She had smelled the odor of bodies being roasted, of putrefied blood, of warm hearts extinguished after the worms had turned them into corpses. She had lived with hell and it had clung to her like a tattoo sticking to the skin.

Then, little by little, the light began to penetrate her. Maryam came to her like a gentle burst of light, setting her free from her previous condition without her knowing, or even being aware of her at all.

She carried her on a new journey of collisions. It was true that it was gentler, but it was also extremely painful for the new frame that she had put on. In her childhood Maryam seemed to have been fashioned from fire. She was a little creature who never stopped quarreling and making mischief, at least so long as she was out of sight of other people — though in front of them, she assumed the spirit of an angel, eager for looks of approval.

She would constantly climb the mulberry, mango, and sycamore trees, then fall off them. Her face would hit the ground and her blood would mingle with the earth but she would never stop what she was doing.

She found this suffering agreeable, as she consigned the other girl to her dark memories. More than once she tried to stop her, but she wasn't helped by her limited potential, which decreed that she should remain in the shadows. So she stored up her grudges that had begun to form.

No, to be honest, this is just a pure lie. She had almost no feelings, she knew neither love nor hatred, and this was her private hell. Feelings that cannot be contradicted are mankind's secret, the place where his superiority lies. Being deprived of them was her death spot, her private Achilles' heel. She wouldn't behave like Grenouille, the hero of Perfume, a novel that Maryam had read and become crazy about. She wouldn't embark on an epic journey with the aim of 'perfuming' her feelings as he had done when he embarked on a journey to find a smell that suited him. Her aim was different. She had to exploit the one wish she had been able to nurture: the desire to escape, to finally leave her dilemma behind her, the maze whose frightening walls she had been left to bang herself against from time immemorial without the slightest mercy.

And she had to do that alone.

Maryam and the others had had no hand in her tragedy. Their two fates, contradictory and united at the same time, were what would decide the struggle.

I t is said that on the evening of the first Thursday of every month someone appears in the palace garden. He emerges from the clumps of English carnations and walks as though he were crossing a fine hair separating heaven from hell. He holds a black stick and wanders slowly among the plants, before being swallowed up by the apple trees planted in the eastern part of the garden.

It sometimes happens that while someone is sitting, apparently thinking of fateful decisions, he is surprised by a face that he feels is familiar. It may be a face like an old friend's, for example, or perhaps some hypothetical ideal of a face that he has perforce tried to create, persuading himself that it is someone who has slipped from the memories of recent years to occupy the present moment—a moment that he has been wanting to appear exceptional in front of his neighbors.

The girl of about eighteen walked timidly into the metro carriage, pursing her lips in an instinctive movement to conceal a needless embarrassment that still dogged her as an inheritance from her childhood years. Maryam's eyes clung involuntarily to the girl's face. The girl's look, afraid of Maryam's eyes that were focused on her, turned her immediately into Edith . . . Edith Malak Munir, whose father had wanted her to be strong as a man, to compensate him for his inability to father a son to help him with his beekeeping. The girl, though, had become plain 'Dithu'—the 'Dithu' who was always in a state for no obvious reason, 'Dithu' with the sweet laugh and the boneless body, as Maryam liked to describe her. Her way of walking had the appearance of a gentle rocking, as if her body lacked a backbone to hold it in balance. She moved like a ghost, with no self-confidence, so that if you saw her coming toward you, you wouldn't know whether she was really coming or getting ready to retreat at any convenient opportunity.

The timid 'metro girl' with the plaited hair, bronze complexion, and teeth clamped in a metal brace, who made heroic, desperate attempts to retain her composure in the face of unknown eyes that scrutinized her unmercifully—for a brief moment, that girl seemed to Maryam like a fine thread joining her to Edith, her childhood friend who had lived like her shadow. Before, that is, she had turned into a shadow of the dark, handsome youth she had run away with, unknown to Maryam, her father, the church and everyone else.

Edith—like Saleh and Nur, and like Yahya and Radwa later— was a thread joining Maryam to life. To the world outside the oppressive palace.

She shared with Maryam, the child then the young girl, most of her memories. One day long ago she had dragged her off to look at the beehives in the middle of the clover fields, and when she was stung by an agitated bee had put mud on the place of the sting so that it would not swell up. Maryam had felt disgusted but had not objected, so as not to give her friend a golden opportunity to make fun of her spoiled lifestyle.

They would slip out together to where Malak stored the honey. They would ignore the jars of honey and head straight for the wooden frames that held the honeycombs. They would steal a frame and take it secretly to the palace, where they would sit in an out-of-the-way place in the garden. With the help of a sharp knife and the experience she had acquired from her beekeeping father, Edith would proceed to release the comb from the frame with the wires attached to it, and cut it into small pieces which they delighted in chewing. The delicious honey would seep into their mouths and they would feel a pleasure unequalled by any other.

The metro girl seemed to Maryam like a gift sent from heaven, to make her feel that she had not completely lost her memory. That after living in the hell of total oblivion of everything to do with her former life, there were still people for whom she could remember the details of the events connecting them to her.

She woke from her musings and did not find the girl. She tried to kill time by biting her fingernails until she arrived at the station she wanted. She left the metro carriage and cautiously made her way through the mass of people until she got to the street. It seemed almost deserted, so immersed in silence that she could clearly hear the sound of her own footsteps on the asphalt.

A stranger knows the cities better than those born there. He remembers their features, and is familiar with every inch of their streets. His feet cling to the asphalt when he walks over it. He does not expect the city to cast him out far away where there is no one and nothing. The stranger tries harder to belong to the city than those who are native to it, for they have no need to prove anything, but walk on in a neutral way, paying no attention to the finer details of their city, looking at strangers with an almost vulgar politeness that springs from their sense of its great superiority.

This was the dilemma in which Maryam found herself in this city. She tried hard to belong to it. She went to great lengths to acquaint herself with everything that related to it. She learned its history by heart, she formed ties with its cafés, its bars, and with the stones of its buildings. She always felt that the streets were embracing her, even longing for her. So she suffered a terrible disappointment when the city rejected and expelled her. Maryam would look at the faces of those around her and see no one, and no one would see her. People behaved as if she were simply made of air, a vacuum walking on two legs, till she collapsed, unable to continue the dangerous game she had unwittingly embarked upon.

She had reached the address she wanted. She couldn't climb the stairs so she made for the lift and pressed the button for the fifth floor. She left the lift and walked toward the flat she was looking for. She knocked on the door and waited for a short while until a fat woman in her forties opened the door. The look in the woman's eyes was as lazy as lazy could be. Maryam introduced herself and the woman nodded her head and reluctantly invited her in. She began to examine Maryam apprehensively until, without beating about the bush, Maryam asked her about Radwa.

As soon as Maryam had asked the question, the atmosphere became electric. The woman became confused and looked around her as if to check for some hidden observer before denying that she knew where she was. Maryam did not give up. She told the woman that she knew how close the two of them were. After being pressed, the fat woman with the lazy look and pallid smile told her that Radwa had traveled to join her father three years ago. Maryam was about to explode in the woman's face, accusing her of lying, but she pulled herself together and left without once looking behind her.

What the woman had said meant that she had either lost her memory or her reason. How could time have become so horribly confused? Could three years be the same as a week?

During the dark winter nights one can hear, from midnight on, the hooting of the owl nesting in the hollow of the ancient mango tree. Old women say that owls shriek like that when they are thirsty for blood, and only stop when they see it.

Maryam walked along the narrow dirt road leading to the village unable to remember almost anything that had happened to her. Her heart was leaping in her chest with anticipation and her mind was swinging back and forth like a clock pendulum. She didn't know exactly what it was that had brought her back to this place. To put it more precisely, she didn't know how she had dared to come back to it. The dew soaking the grass on either side of the path had left its traces on her shoes and trousers, and her hair was horribly disheveled. She tried to imagine what might be waiting for her there this time, but just to think about it frightened her. She hurried on as if to challenge the thick fog that enveloped the atmosphere. She was coming close to Edith's house on the edge of the village, certain from her last visit that she would not find it, but she soon caught sight of the little house built of white granite that appeared before her in the distance, surrounded by climbing gourds and ivy. Her feet stopped despite herself and she thought of going back, but something stronger than herself made her continue on her way.

Tante Helena was splashing the earth patch in front of the house with the water left over from washing clothes. Maryam greeted her, but the woman did not take the slightest notice. Maryam stopped near her for a minute, but she carried on doing what she was doing without paying any attention to her, so she left her and headed toward the palace, which was still a long way off.

When Maryam passed Kawthar's house and saw her sitting on the cane chair on her balcony, she almost started to run. She didn't want to have to face her, even though she wasn't certain that Kawthar would see her at all.

The paths were as dusty as she had always known them to be, except in front of the houses, where the occupants would zealously sweep the patch opposite them and splash it with water. Animal dung was scattered here and there. The smell of Nile water, slightly putrid as it always was in the morning, permeated the place, and small children with almost no clothes on had started happily chasing each other.

Something inside Maryam told her that she had no place here, but she couldn't go back after getting so close to the key to the maze in which she unwittingly found herself.

Suddenly she lost her self-control. She no longer had the strength to walk. Despite this she went on, as some external force directed her and even moved her feet. She started to float like a delicate bird, moving forward without any noticeable effort.

Finally, she stopped in front of the enormous palace, of which she knew every inch by heart. The gigantic iron gate opened and she went in, terrified. She stepped slowly along the pathway paved with alternating pink and gray marble, gazing at the garden whose trees had been pruned and whose flowers were open again. Someone she didn't know was watering the plants, singing a song of Sharifa Fadil's, she believed. She ignored him and climbed up the marble stairs leading to the spacious terrace surrounded by jasmine shrubs with the delicate, redolent fragrance.

She sat on one of the bamboo chairs with multicolored mattresses that had been tastefully spread around the terrace in an obvious pattern. In the middle of them were some tables, also of bamboo. Only a few minutes went by before a woman appeared who looked exactly like Narges and sat on a chair next to Maryam without taking any notice of the fact that she was there. Maryam called her name but she did not hear. She put her hand on the woman's right arm and felt she was touching a void. She tried to scream but couldn't. No sound came out. She felt completely numb. With the same sense of numbness she left the woman and headed into the palace. She walked from one hall to another and from one corridor to another until she reached the wing where Yusif and Narges lived. She found Yusif, who had just finished his breakfast and begun to drink his morning coffee. He was holding the cup with his good arm as he fondled a small child sitting beside him. A girl with brown hair and honey-colored eyes. Maryam fell down in a faint. All the sounds around her vanished and changed into a scream like the hooting of an owl, drowning out everything else in pitch darkness.

When she woke she found herself lying on a piece of ground planted with clover, watered two days ago at most. Her clothes were damp with a green stain and the distinctive smell of clover. She got up with difficulty and examined her clothes in despair. She walked on without thinking, in no particular direction. The whole place was strange to her. A spot next to the Nile, planted with clover and fava beans, with a small area next to it full of mature camphor trees, so closely planted that someone looking from a distance would think he was seeing the tangled branches of a forest.

Maryam left the spot, dragging her feet with difficulty. After half an hour's walk she reached a narrow dirt track, surrounded on both sides by land about ten meters lower that had been overgrown by alfalfa and bamboo. As she walked along the narrow track she felt that she was in danger of falling into the swamp of vegetation at any moment. Then, at last, the house appeared before her in the distance.

She approached it gradually. It looked exactly as she had known it before, a building made of clay surrounded by a small courtyard with a tall palm in the center and a fence of dry rushes around it. She went into the courtyard timidly and made for the broken-down wooden door. She saw a hand stain of blood on it. She put her own hand on it and it was a perfect match. The door opened and she went in, to be met by an almost total darkness. She closed her eyes for a moment and when she opened them there were some faint rays of light that had gradually begun to penetrate.

Glossary

bango: Inexpensive type of marijuana grown mainly in Egypt and Sudan.

Fatiha: The opening chapter, or sura, of the Quran.

fedayeen: Commandos, freedom-fighters.

feddan: Land measure equal to 1.038 acres.

fellaheen: Peasants.

gallabiya: Traditional Egyptian full-length loose gown, worn by both men and women.

Mahallawi: From, or made in, al-Mahalla al-Kubra, a town in the Egyptian Delta famous for its textile factories.

pasha: Formerly a title of high-ranking officers, now also used as a form of address suggesting familiarity.

shaykha: Feminine of shaykh (also sheikh), a title used of an elder or religious person or, more generally, to indicate respect; also used, as here, sarcastically.

shisha: A water pipe for smoking tobacco or marijuana.

Translator's Note

Mansoura Ez Eldin was born in 1976 in a small village in the Egyptian Delta. She graduated with a degree in journalism from Cairo University in 1998 and first started publishing short stories in the Arab press when she was twenty-one. She has worked in Egyptian television, and presently runs the book review section of the Egyptian literary magazine *Akhbar al-adab*.

Mansoura Ez Eldin's first collection of short stories, entitled *Daw' muhtazz (Flickering Light)*, was published in Cairo in 2001 by the newly established publishing house Merit Press; five stories from this collection have been translated into English and were published in *Unbuttoning the Violin* (Banipal Books, 2006). *Matahat Maryam (Maryam's Maze)*, the author's first novel, was first published in Arabic by Merit Press in 2004; extracts from the present English translation were published in an earlier version in *Banipal* issue 25 (Spring 2006). She is currently working on a second novel.

Readers of *Maryam's Maze* who are already familiar with the author's short stories will quickly feel themselves at home in this more extended work, which again reveals the author's preoccupation with the relationship between dreams and reality, and by the influence of the past on the present. Set in the house of Yusif el Tagi, where much of the story's action unfolds, this enigmatic novel relates the story of a woman struggling to find her way through the confusion of the world around her. As the narrative meanders through the histories and relationships of the various characters, Mansoura Ez Eldin tells a story that on one level touches on universal human emotions. At the same time, however, the inner maze of dreams and memories in which the young Maryam finds herself is clearly rooted in the political and social realities of modern Egyptian life. Particularly striking in terms of literary technique is the author's use of the idea of the *qarin* or *qarina*, or 'spirit companion,' a concept found in the Qur'an but which undoubtedly has its origins in pre-Islamic times. Transformed by the author into Maryam's 'double,' the device provides a vivid illustration of how the cultural heritage of the region is being incorporated into modern literary techniques.

In *Maryam's Maze*, Mansoura Ez Eldin has woven a haunting allegorical tale with a distinctive personal vision that represents a unique contribution to the corpus of contemporary Egyptian fiction. The precision of language of the work at times poses a considerable challenge to the translator, and I am therefore particularly grateful to the author for her constant readiness to help with the elucidation of troublesome passages. I am also grateful to the staff of the American University in Cairo Press, in particular Neil Hewison, Nadia Naqib, and Wiam El-Tamami for their constant support and encouragement throughout the period of the translation.

Modern Arabic Literature
from the American University in Cairo Press

Ibrahim Abdel Meguid *Birds of Amber* • *Distant Train*
No One Sleeps in Alexandria • *The Other Place*
Yahya Taher Abdullah *The Collar and the Bracelet* • *The Mountain of Green Tea*
Leila Abouzeid *The Last Chapter*
Hamdi Abu Golayyel *A Dog with No Tail* • *Thieves in Retirement*
Yusuf Abu Rayya *Wedding Night*
Ahmed Alaidy *Being Abbas el Abd*
Idris Ali *Dongola* • *Poor*
Radwa Ashour *Granada*
Ibrahim Aslan *The Heron* • *Nile Sparrows*
Alaa Al Aswany *Chicago* • *Friendly Fire* • *The Yacoubian Building*
Fadhil al-Azzawi *Cell Block Five* • *The Last of the Angels*
Ali Bader *Papa Sartre*
Liana Badr *The Eye of the Mirror*
Hala El Badry *A Certain Woman* • *Muntaha*
Salwa Bakr *The Golden Chariot* • *The Man from Bashmour*
The Wiles of Men
Halim Barakat *The Crane*
Hoda Barakat *Disciples of Passion* • *The Tiller of Waters*
Mourid Barghouti *I Saw Ramallah*
Mohamed Berrada *Like a Summer Never to Be Repeated*
Mohamed El-Bisatie *Clamor of the Lake*
Houses Behind the Trees • *Hunger*
A Last Glass of Tea • *Over the Bridge*
Mahmoud Darwish *The Butterfly's Burden*
Tarek Eltayeb *Cities without Palms*
Mansoura Ez Eldin *Maryam's Maze*
Ibrahim Farghali *The Smiles of the Saints*
Hamdy el-Gazzar *Black Magic*
Fathy Ghanem *The Man Who Lost His Shadow*
Randa Ghazy *Dreaming of Palestine*
Gamal al-Ghitani *Pyramid Texts* • *The Zafarani Files* • *Zayni Barakat*
Tawfiq al-Hakim *The Essential Tawfiq al-Hakim*
Yahya Hakki *The Lamp of Umm Hashim*
Abdelilah Hamdouchi *The Final Bet*
Bensalem Himmich *The Polymath* • *The Theocrat*
Taha Hussein *The Days* • *A Man of Letters* • *The Sufferers*
Sonallah Ibrahim *Cairo: From Edge to Edge* • *The Committee* • *Zaat*
Yusuf Idris *City of Love and Ashes* • *The Essential Yusuf Idris*
Denys Johnson-Davies *The AUC Press Book of Modern Arabic Literature*
In a Fertile Desert: Modern Writing from the United Arab Emirates
Under the Naked Sky: Short Stories from the Arab World
Said al-Kafrawi *The Hill of Gypsies*

Sahar Khalifeh *The End of Spring*
The Image, the Icon, and the Covenant • *The Inheritance*
Edwar al-Kharrat *Rama and the Dragon* • *Stones of Bobello*
Betool Khedairi *Absent*
Mohammed Khudayyir *Basrayatha*
Ibrahim al-Koni *Anubis* • *Gold Dust* • *The Seven Veils of Seth*
Naguib Mahfouz *Adrift on the Nile* • *Akhenaten: Dweller in Truth*
Arabian Nights and Days • *Autumn Quail* • *Before the Throne* • *The Beggar*
The Beginning and the End • *Cairo Modern*
The Cairo Trilogy: Palace Walk, Palace of Desire, Sugar Street
Children of the Alley • *The Day the Leader Was Killed*
The Dreams • *Dreams of Departure* • *Echoes of an Autobiography*
The Harafish • *The Journey of Ibn Fattouma* • *Karnak Café*
Khan al-Khalili • *Khufu's Wisdom* • *Life's Wisdom* • *Midaq Alley*
The Mirage • *Miramar* • *Mirrors* • *Morning and Evening Talk*
Naguib Mahfouz at Sidi Gaber • *Respected Sir* • *Rhadopis of Nubia*
The Search • *The Seventh Heaven* • *Thebes at War*
The Thief and the Dogs • *The Time and the Place*
Voices from the Other World • *Wedding Song*
Mohamed Makhzangi *Memories of a Meltdown*
Alia Mamdouh *The Loved Ones* • *Naphtalene*
Selim Matar *The Woman of the Flask*
Ibrahim al-Mazini *Ten Again*
Yousef Al-Mohaimeed *Wolves of the Crescent Moon*
Ahlam Mosteghanemi *Chaos of the Senses* • *Memory in the Flesh*
Shakir Mustafa *Contemporary Iraqi Fiction: An Anthology*
Mohamed Mustagab *Tales from Dayrut*
Buthaina Al Nasiri *Final Night*
Ibrahim Nasrallah *Inside the Night*
Haggag Hassan Oddoul *Nights of Musk*
Mohamed Mansi Qandil *Moon over Samarqand*
Abd al-Hakim Qasim *Rites of Assent*
Somaya Ramadan *Leaves of Narcissus*
Lenin El-Ramly *In Plain Arabic*
Mekkawi Said *Cairo Swan Song*
Ghada Samman *The Night of the First Billion*
Mahdi Issa al-Saqr *East Winds, West Winds*
Rafik Schami *Damascus Nights* • *The Dark Side of Love*
Khairy Shalaby *The Hashish Waiter* • *The Lodging House*
Miral al-Tahawy *Blue Aubergine* • *Gazelle Tracks* • *The Tent*
Bahaa Taher *As Doha Said* • *Love in Exile*
Fuad al-Takarli *The Long Way Back*
Zakaria Tamer *The Hedgehog*
M.M. Tawfik *Murder in the Tower of Happiness*
Mahmoud Al-Wardani *Heads Ripe for Plucking*
Latifa al-Zayyat *The Open Door*